LITTLE HEDGEHOG
BOOKS

MEMASAURUS AND ME

I love my Memasaurus.
She is very special!

When we are together, we like to act silly and stomp around.

Memasaurus is always impressed by my loud roar... even when I'm a little *too* loud.

Sometimes, Memasaurus tells me "No."

But I know that it's only to keep me safe.

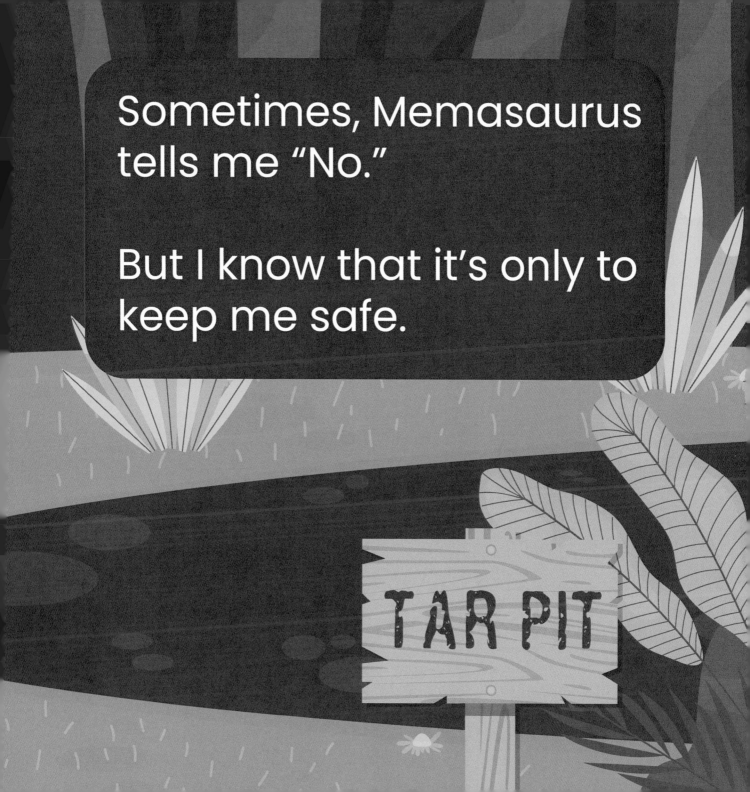

At the beach, she makes me wear a hat so I don't get sunburned. (But she wears one too.)

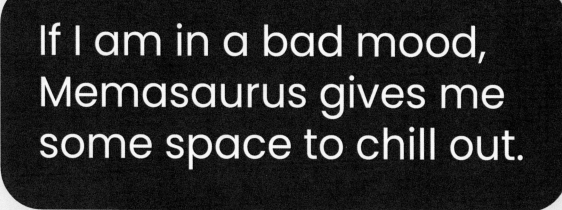

If I am in a bad mood, Memasaurus gives me some space to chill out.

She worries when I try new things, but she knows that I need to soar when the time is right.

When Memasaurus tucks me in for the night, I feel safe and snuggly because I know she's near me.

Made in the USA
Las Vegas, NV
02 January 2025

15634521R00021